AF604137

Race to the South Pole

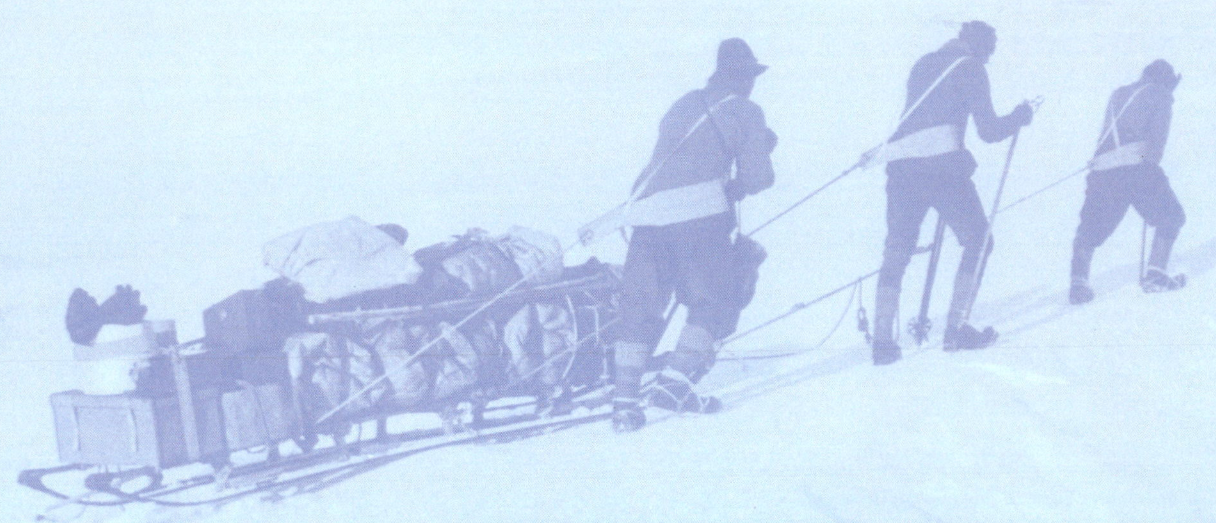

Alan Trussell-Cullen

Daniel Atkinson

NELSON CENGAGE Learning

Australia • Brazil • Japan • Korea • Mexico • Singapore • Spain • United Kingdom • United States

Race to the South Pole

Text: Alan Trussell-Cullen
Illustrations: Daniel Atkinson
Editor: Rebecca Crisp
Design: Karen Mayo
Series design: James Lowe
Photo researcher: Corrina Tauschke
Production controller: Adam Bextream
Reprint: Siew Han Ong

Acknowledgements
The author and publisher would like to acknowledge permission to reproduce material from the following sources:
akg-images: p. 3; Corbis/Bettmann: pp. 6–7, 8 (right), back cover; Getty Images: pp. 1, 7 (top), 9, 10 (main), 11, cover; National Library of Australia: p. 10 (inset); Photolibrary: p. 7 (bottom); Photolibrary/Bridgeman Art Library: p. 4; Photolibrary/Science Photo Library/US Library of Congress: pp. 5, 8 (left).

Every effort has been made to trace and acknowledge copyright. However, if any infringement has occurred, the publishers tender their apologies and invite the copyright holders to contact them.

Fast Forward Independent Texts
Level 24

For product information and technology assistance,
in Australia call 1300 790 853;
in New Zealand call 0508 635 766

For permission to use material from this text or product,
please email **aust.permissions@cengage.com**

ISBN 978 0 17 017945 4
ISBN 978 0 17 017899 0 (set)

Cengage Learning Australia
Level 7, 80 Dorcas Street
South Melbourne, Victoria Australia 3205

Cengage Learning New Zealand
Unit 4B Rosedale Office Park
331 Rosedale Road, Albany, North Shore NZ 0632

For learning solutions, visit **cengage.com.au**

Printed in Australia by Ligare Pty Ltd
2 3 4 5 6 7 23 22 21 20 19

Race to the South Pole

Alan Trussell-Cullen

Daniel Atkinson

Contents

A New Continent

By the late nineteenth century, all the continents except Antarctica had been explored. Explorers knew about a remote continent that they called the 'Unknown Southern Land', because many sailors had seen land as they travelled the southern oceans to avoid bad weather.

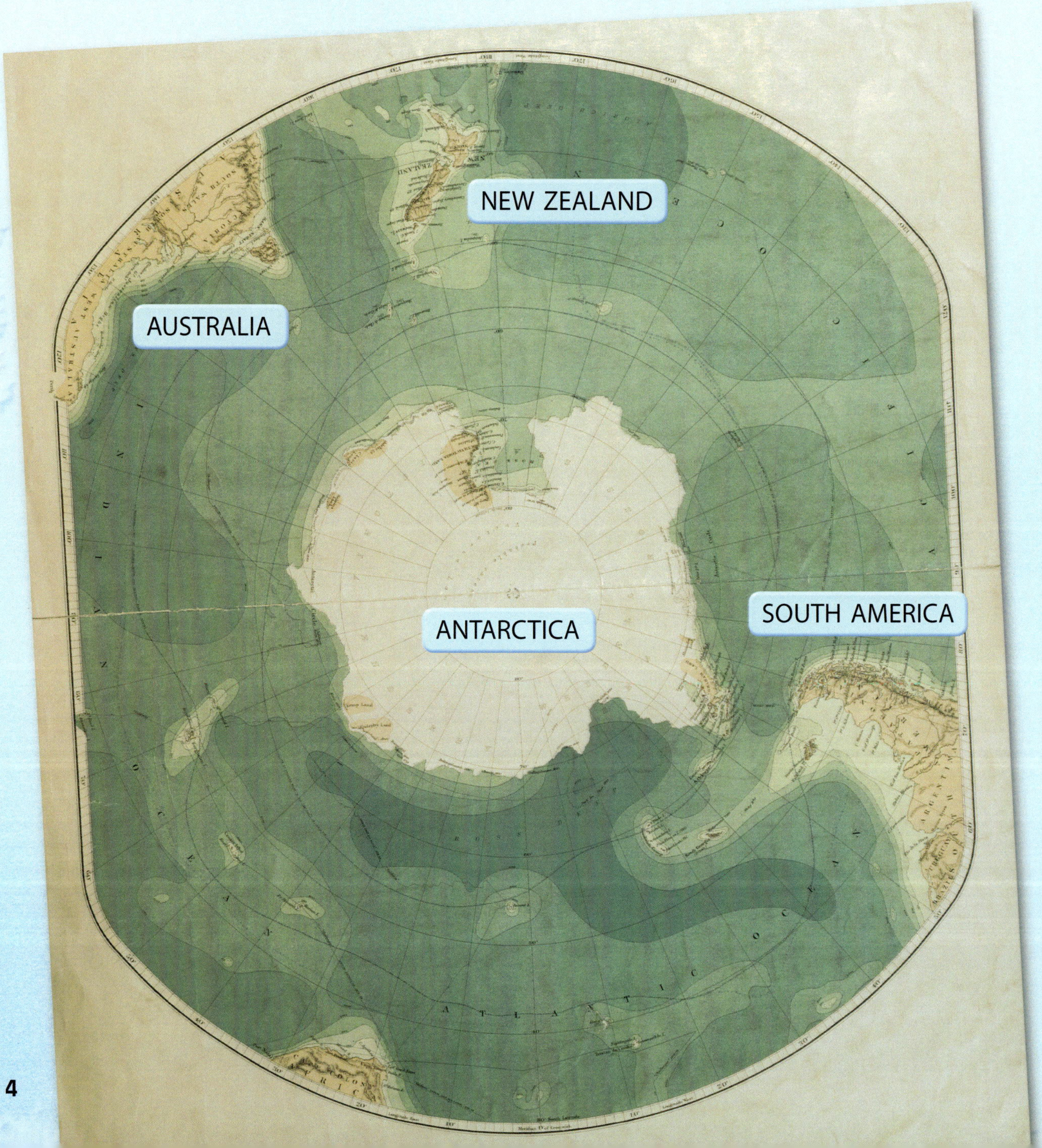

NEW ZEALAND
AUSTRALIA
ANTARCTICA
SOUTH AMERICA

Part of the coastline had been mapped by these explorers, and gradually a new continent was taking shape. This continent was eventually named Antarctica.

The waters of Antarctica were rich with sea life, and many people who were keen to make a good living set off into the southern oceans to hunt seals and whales.

sailors hunting whales

By the beginning of the twentieth century, no fewer than seven countries were planning scientific **expeditions** to Antarctica. Each team wanted to gather knowledge of the area in order to claim new land for their own country.

Each country realised that the greatest prize was to be the first to reach the South Pole, which was considered the most **remote** place on Earth. But due to the **extreme** cold and difficult environment of the area, it was a few years before explorers were successful in reaching the South Pole.

In 1909, British explorer Ernest Shackleton and his team were the first people to come close to the South Pole.

Shackleton and some of his team

Shackleton's ship, stuck in the ice

Two Expeditions

Captain Robert Scott was a British explorer who visited Antarctica between 1901 and 1904. On that trip, his team managed to get within 160 kilometres of the South Pole, but sickness forced the men to return.

Scott was keen to try again, as he knew a team from Norway was planning to attempt the journey as well, under the direction of Roald Amundsen.

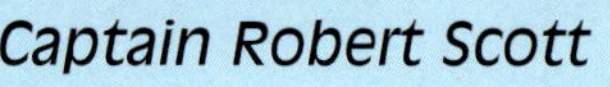

Captain Robert Scott

Roald Amundsen

Captain Scott's team on their way to Antarctica

Scott organised a team of men and collected the equipment and supplies necessary for the trip. He left England in June 1910, and after stopping off in Australia, he learned that Amundsen and his team were heading south at the same time.

There were important differences in the way the two teams prepared for the journey. Scott made the mistake of using horses and motorised sleds to carry food and equipment. He soon learned that neither the machines nor the animals were suited to such an extreme environment. Some of the horses died, and the men had to drag the broken-down sleds.

the horses used on Scott's expedition

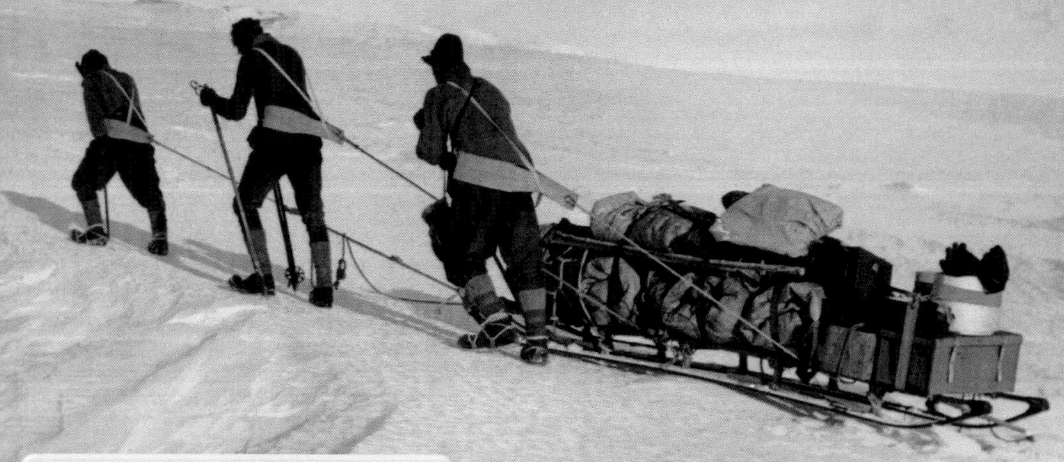

Scott's men dragging a sled

one of Amundsen's dog teams

Amundsen and his men used well-trained dog teams. The dogs were used to transport food supplies to different locations on the way to the South Pole before Amundsen's team began their journey. During the journey, the dogs pulled the supply sleds, and some of them even became food for the men and the other dogs.

Amundsen's team also had good equipment and more suitable clothing, and some of his team were good skiers.

The scene was set for an exciting race.

Robert Scott's Team

- Lawrence Oates
- Edward Wilson
- Henry Bowers
- Edgar Evans

Roald Amundsen's Team

- Olav Bjaaland
- Oscar Wisting
- Helmer Hanssen
- Sverre Hassel

CHAPTER 2

The Race Is On

IN 1911, TWO TEAMS BEGAN A RACE TO THE SOUTH POLE. CAPTAIN ROBERT SCOTT'S TEAM CAME FROM BRITAIN. ROALD AMUNDSEN'S TEAM CAME FROM NORWAY.

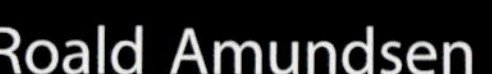

Roald Amundsen

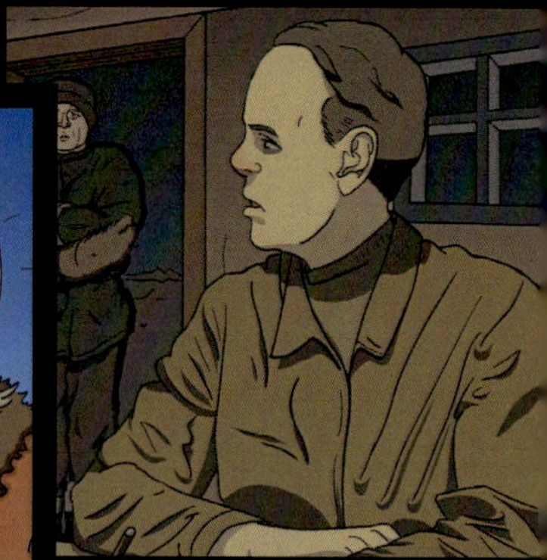

Captain Robert Scott

JANUARY 1911: SCOTT SET UP HIS CAMP.

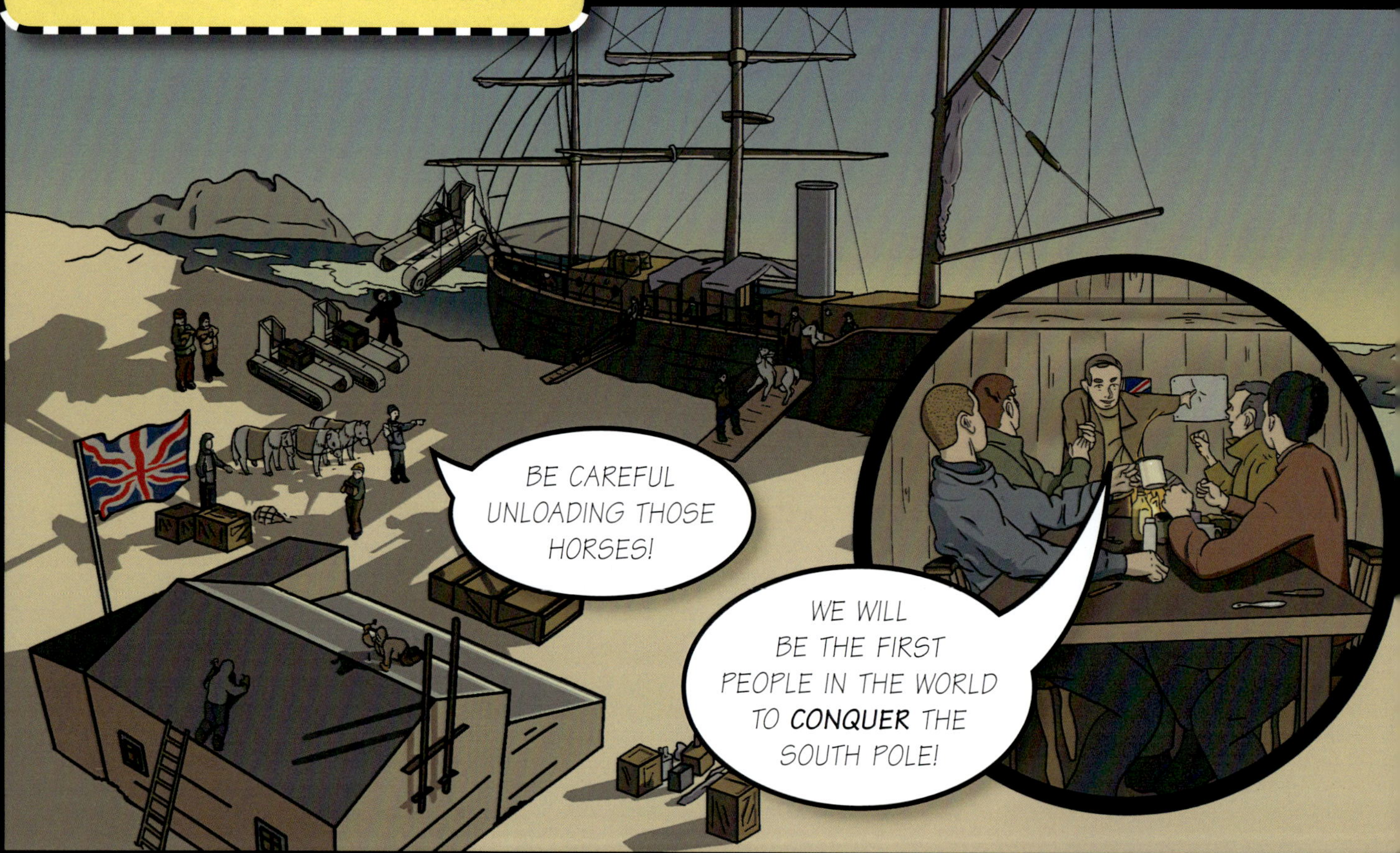

BE CAREFUL UNLOADING THOSE HORSES!

WE WILL BE THE FIRST PEOPLE IN THE WORLD TO **CONQUER** THE SOUTH POLE!

AMUNDSEN SET UP HIS CAMP. EACH TEAM BROUGHT READY-TO-BUILD CABINS.

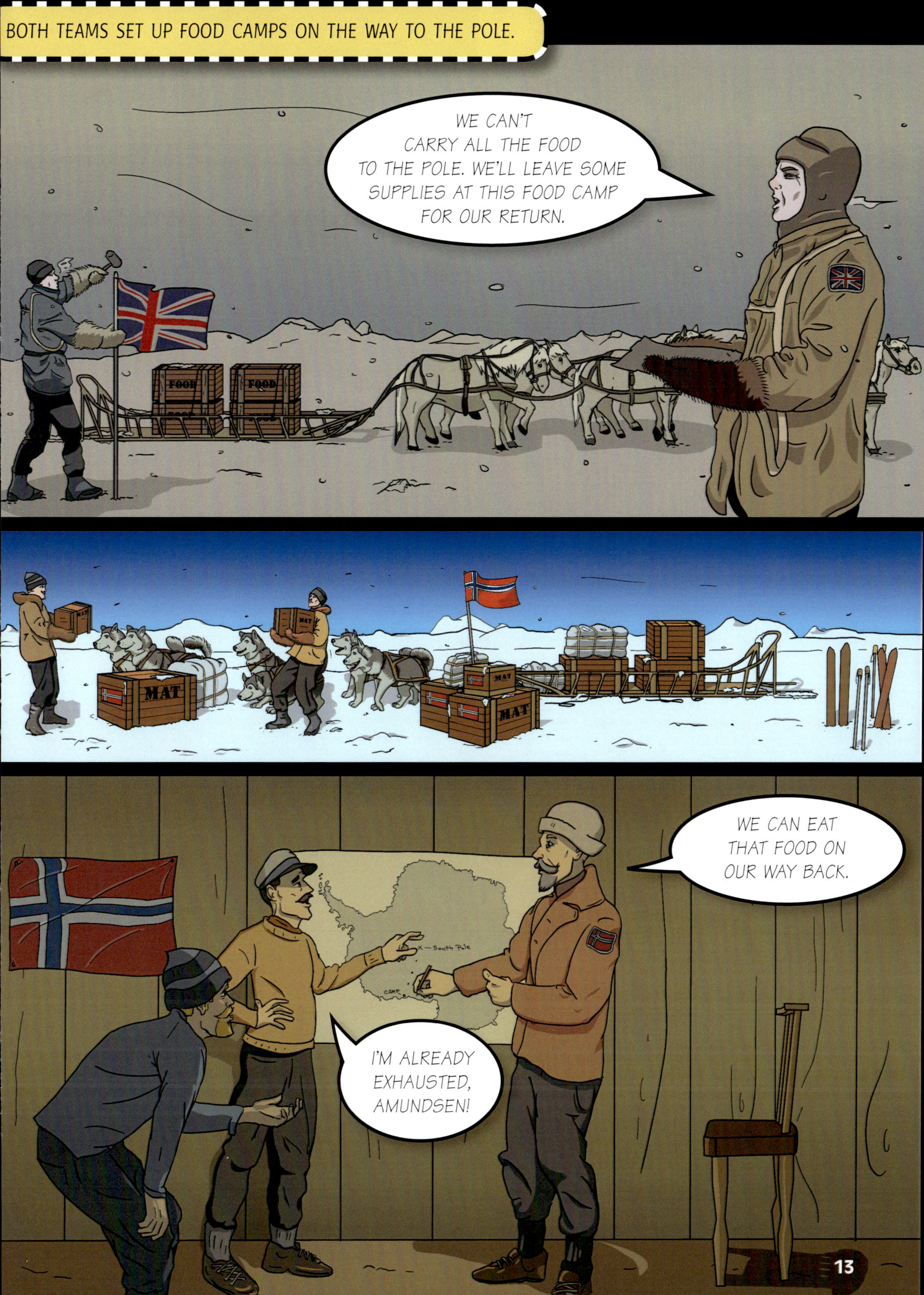

BOTH TEAMS SET UP FOOD CAMPS ON THE WAY TO THE POLE.

WE CAN'T CARRY ALL THE FOOD TO THE POLE. WE'LL LEAVE SOME SUPPLIES AT THIS FOOD CAMP FOR OUR RETURN.

WE CAN EAT THAT FOOD ON OUR WAY BACK.

I'M ALREADY EXHAUSTED, AMUNDSEN!

WINTER ARRIVED. THE WEATHER WAS EXTREME.
I'M FREEZING, SCOTT! IT'S WILD OUT THERE!
THIS IS WINTER IN THE COLDEST PLACE ON EARTH, OATES!
24 May 1911. Winter is one long night here ...
AMUNDSEN'S TEAM WAS MUCH HAPPIER.
YES!
AMUNDSEN WINS AGAIN!

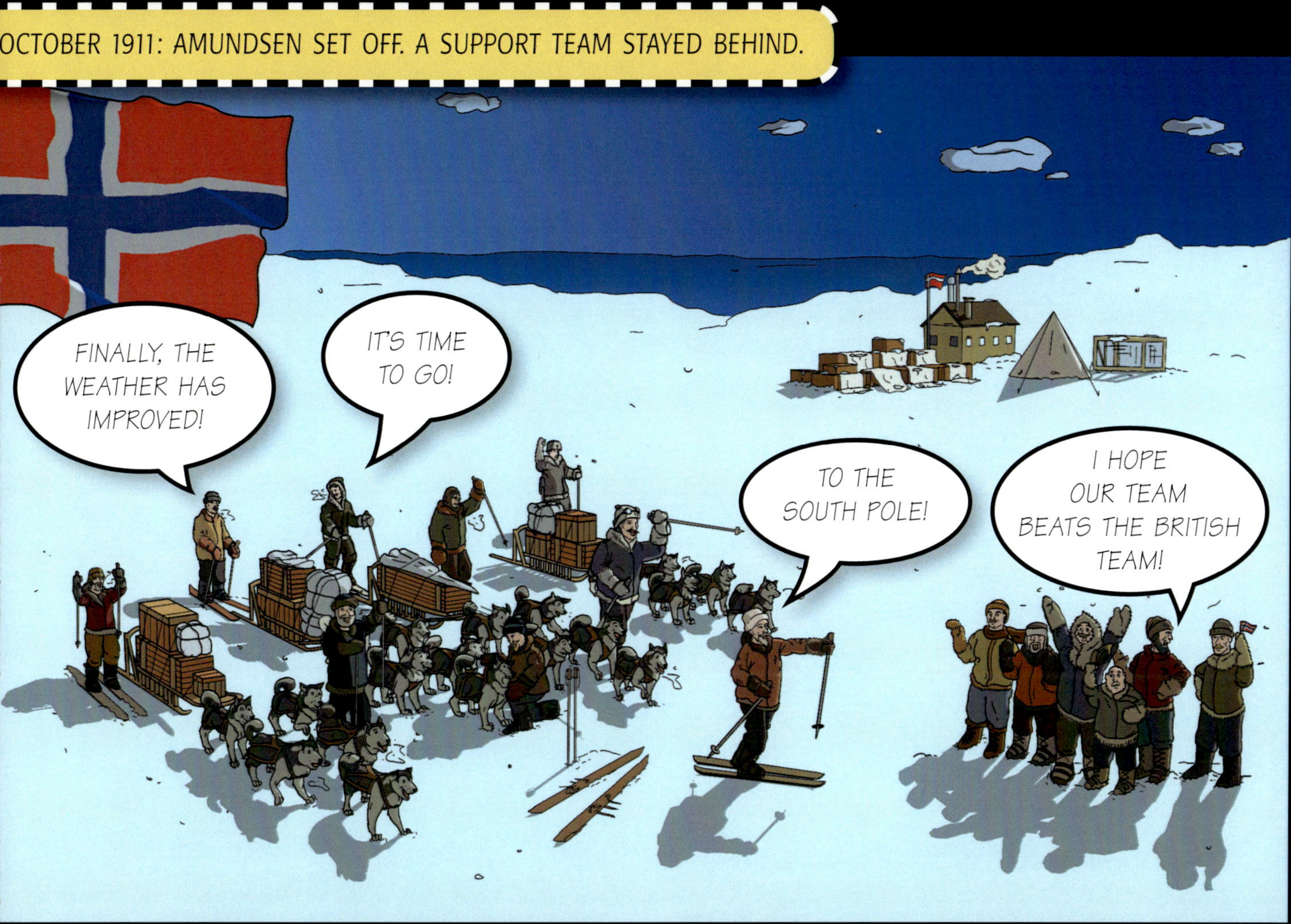

OCTOBER 1911: AMUNDSEN SET OFF. A SUPPORT TEAM STAYED BEHIND.

FINALLY, THE WEATHER HAS IMPROVED!

IT'S TIME TO GO!

TO THE SOUTH POLE!

I HOPE OUR TEAM BEATS THE BRITISH TEAM!

NOVEMBER 1911: SCOTT SET OFF. SCOTT'S HORSES DID NOT LIKE THE NOISE OF THE MOTORISED SLEDS.

THESE MOTOR SLEDS SHOULD MAKE THINGS EASIER FOR US!

RRRR!

IT'S OK!

RRRR!

TO THE SOUTH POLE!

AMUNDSEN'S TEAM MADE GOOD PROGRESS.

BUT THERE WERE DANGERS ...

SCOTT HAD PROBLEMS. SOME OF HIS MEN RETURNED TO CAMP.

THREE WEEKS LATER ...
DO WE HAVE TO GO OVER THAT MOUNTAIN RANGE, AMUNDSEN?
WE CAN FIND A WAY!
HOW ... MUCH ... FURTHER ... TO ... THE ... POLE?
WE CAN'T ... GIVE ... UP ... NOW.
SCOTT'S SITUATION WORSENED.
THE HORSES!
THERE GOES MOST OF OUR FOOD, SCOTT!
WE NEED TO RECOVER THAT FOOD!
THERE'S NO MORE ROPE!
PULL HIM BACK UP.
I CAN'T REACH IT!
LATER ...
THE HORSES ARE NOT DOING WELL. THEY ARE NOT USED TO THIS COLD!
WE MUST PUT THEM DOWN.
SHOULD WE TURN BACK?
WE WILL NEVER TURN BACK. WE WILL PULL THE SLEDS OURSELVES.

14 DECEMBER 1911: AMUNDSEN WON THE RACE TO THE SOUTH POLE.

WE HAVE MADE IT! THIS IS THE SOUTH POLE!

WE DID IT!
WE DID IT FOR NORWAY!

17 JANUARY 1912: SCOTT ARRIVED AT THE SOUTH POLE – TOO LATE.
OH NO ...

THE NORWEGIAN FLAG!
AMUNDSEN WAS FIRST.

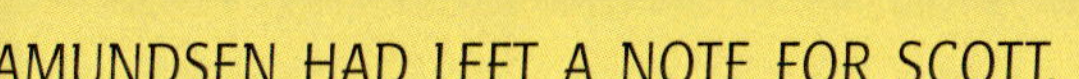
AMUNDSEN HAD LEFT A NOTE FOR SCOTT.

Captain Scott

Dear Captain Scott,
Please send this letter to the King of Norway in case we don't make it back.
Roald Amundsen
King Haakon VII

RETURNING FROM THE POLE, SCOTT'S MEN WERE NOT COPING WELL.
THAT'S THE LAST OF OUR FOOD.
EVANS, KEEP UP! WE HAVE TO KEEP GOING ...
EVANS HAS STOPPED BREATHING ...

25 JANUARY 1912: AMUNDSEN ARRIVED BACK AT HIS CAMP.
OUR CAMP!
OUR SHIP!

WE ARE GOING HOME!

A SNOW STORM HIT SCOTT'S TEAM. OATES, ONE OF THE MEN, COULD NOT GO ON.
MY FINGERS ARE BLACK.

I'M JUST GOING OUTSIDE AND I MAY BE SOME TIME.

OATES DID NOT RETURN.
March 1912.
We knew Oates was walking to his death.
It was the act of a brave man ...

7 MARCH 1912: AMUNDSEN ARRIVED IN HOBART, AUSTRALIA.
WE MADE IT TO THE SOUTH POLE FIRST!
THE NEWS QUICKLY SPREAD AROUND THE WORLD.
BEEP! BEEP!
AMUNDSEN HAS DONE IT!
The New York Times
AMUNDSEN FIRST TO THE SOUTH POLE!
The Oslo Herald
NORWEGIAN WINS ANTARCTIC RACE!
London Evening News
NO SIGN OF CAPTAIN SCOTT

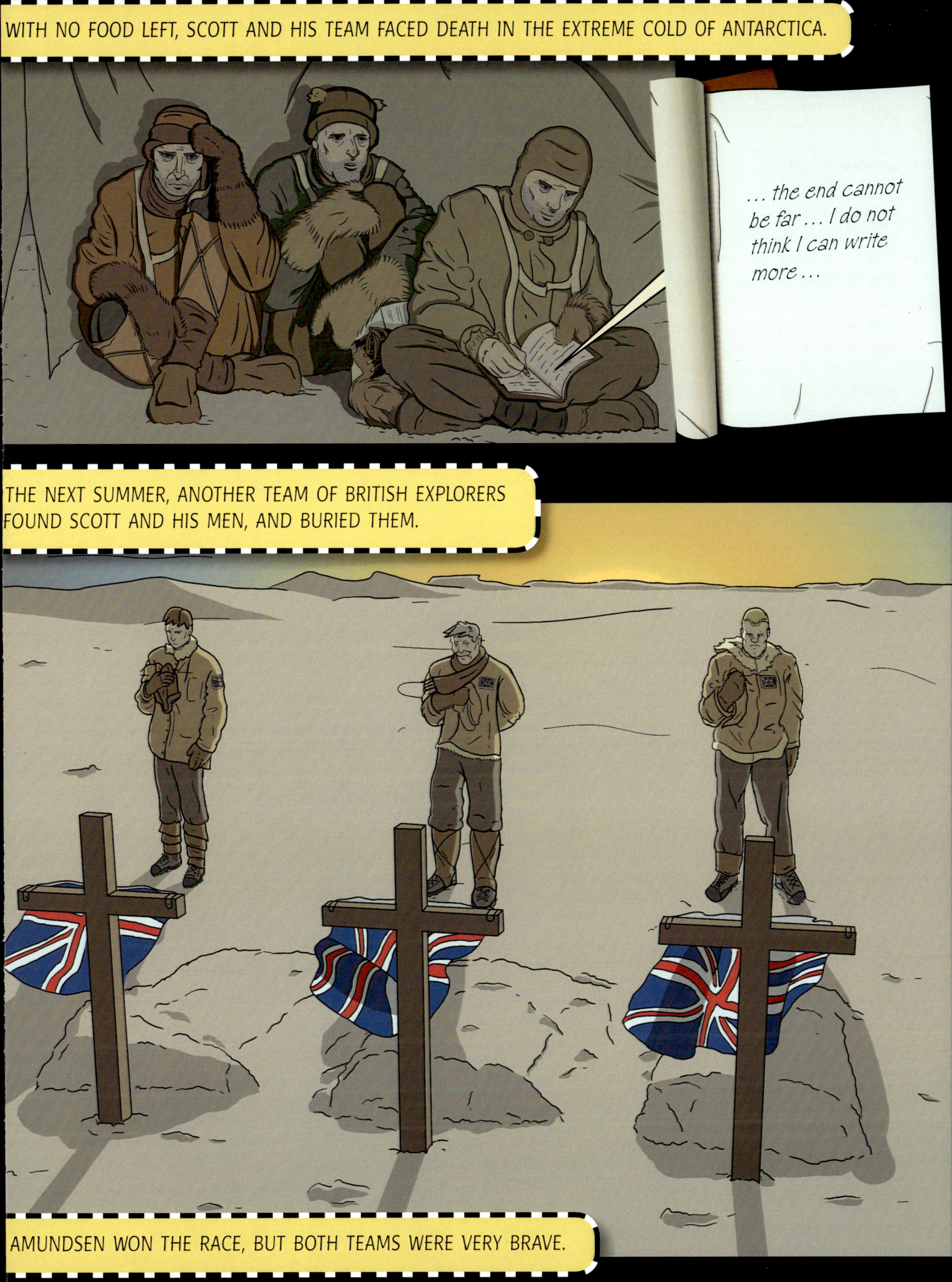

WITH NO FOOD LEFT, SCOTT AND HIS TEAM FACED DEATH IN THE EXTREME COLD OF ANTARCTICA.

THE NEXT SUMMER, ANOTHER TEAM OF BRITISH EXPLORERS FOUND SCOTT AND HIS MEN, AND BURIED THEM.

AMUNDSEN WON THE RACE, BUT BOTH TEAMS WERE VERY BRAVE.

Glossary

abandon to leave behind

conquer to gain through great effort

crevasse a deep opening in the ice of a glacier

expeditions journeys made for some specific purpose

extreme well beyond average

remote far away

Index